Insects Galore

A collection of six stories

Written by Katiuscia Giusti

Illustrations by Agnes Lemaire, Color by Doug Calder

ISBN 13: 978-3-03730-095-4

www.auroraproduction.com

Drudy's Day

Tristan's sob could be heard loud and clear through the house and garden.

"What's wrong, Tristan?" Grandpa Jake asked, as he came to find his grandson tending to a small, bleeding cut on his knee. "Oh dear, it looks like you had a little accident."

"It hurts real bad, Grandpa," Tristan said, through his tears.

"I'm sure it does. I'm so sorry."

"Hmm," Grandpa Jake said suddenly, "I think I just found the cause of this accident. Look at this. Your shoelaces weren't tied, and you must have tripped over them."

"Oh, I guess I did forget to tie them," Tristan confessed. "I was in a race with my friend to see who would get

outside
the quickest,
and I must have
forgotten."

"Well, it wasn't so quick
after all, because you ended
up getting hurt. You know what,
though? This reminds me of a story about little Drudy."

"Drudy?" Tristan asked, as he brushed his tears aside.

"Yes, Drudy was a dragonfly who had a little accident just like you did—and she learned some very good lessons through it."

"Please tell me, Grandpa," Tristan said eagerly.

"It all happened one day when Drudy found her friends, Lincoln and Fiery…" Grandpa Jake began.

— ♦ —

"You'll never believe what happened to me," Drudy panted, coming up to where her best friends were relaxing in the sun.

"Tell us, please," Lincoln said.
"You sure look tired," Fiery added. "You must've been flying for miles."

"Not really, but I just had a scary accident. I'll tell you all about it."

Fiery fluttered down to perch on a dandelion leaf, while Lincoln settled himself comfortably nearby. They both were eager to hear Drudy's tale.

"It was so warm this morning that I decided to visit my dragonfly friends at the pond," Drudy began. "We were playing flying games. It was a lot of fun. First we'd fly up as high as we could, and then we'd dive down real fast. We were seeing who could make it to the surface of the water and catch one of the mosquitoes circling the surface of the pond without getting wet."

"I wasn't doing so good," Drudy confessed. "I could fly high, but I wasn't able to dive as quickly as the others, so I was hardly catching any mosquitoes. I started getting frustrated because the other dragonflies were constantly winning.

"I got angry
and wanted to
prove that I could be
as good as the rest of them.
Plus, I didn't want anyone to
think I was scared of getting stuck in
the water, or worried about my wings getting wet."

"I wasn't being careful at all, and I went real high
and decided to dive as fast as I could. I picked up so
much speed when I was diving that I wasn't able to turn
and catch the mosquito. Instead, I hit the water with a
splash," Drudy explained. "I landed so fast that I felt like

everything around me was spinning. My friends hovered above me, asking if I was okay. I said I was fine, but when I tried to get out of the water I couldn't."

"That's terrible!" Fiery exclaimed.

"You must have been scared," Lincoln said. "I would've been."

"At first I wasn't scared, but then I started to get a bit worried when I realized that I couldn't fly out."

"My wings were so wet and heavy; I couldn't lift them. I was stuck."

"Oh dear!" Lincoln said with a worried look on his face.

"What happened next?" Fiery asked curiously.

"I thought I might be stuck in the water for a very long time and maybe even drown. My friends decided to go try and find help, so they flew away. When I was alone I felt very helpless."

"What did you do?" Lincoln asked.

"I remembered what my mom had always told me to do if I found myself in a difficult situation: I prayed. I asked God to help my friends find some way of helping me, or that God would send someone to rescue me. I told Him that I'd be more careful next time and not get so competitive."

"And?" Fiery interrupted.
"Just then two children
were walking by the pond.

They had caught a frog in their yard and were bringing it to the pond to set it free. I tried calling for help, but they didn't see or hear me. So I prayed again, and then the little girl saw me."

"'Cid, Cid!' she shouted. 'There's a dragonfly in the water. It looks like it needs help.'"

"Her brother turned around and saw me, and he gently fished me out of the water."

"'Poor little thing,' he said. I had swallowed some water too, because I'd been in the water for quite some time. 'Good thing you saw the dragonfly, Sheila,' he told his sister. 'I don't know how much longer it would've lasted in the water. Let's put it on this leaf here so that

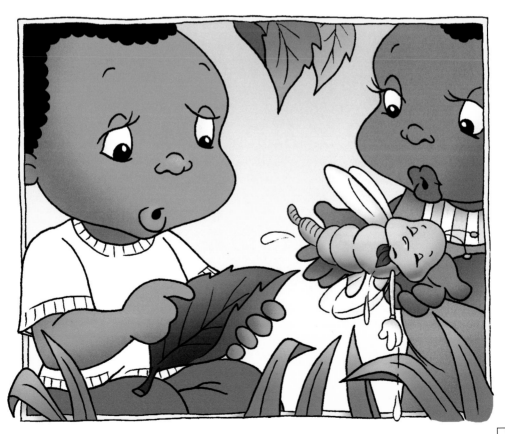

the sun can dry its wings,
and then it'll be able to fly again.'"

"'Yes, let's do that,' Sheila replied."

"It's so good that those kids were there when you
needed them," Fiery said.

"That must've been so scary, but I'm so glad that you're
alright now," Lincoln sighed.

"Me too," Drudy agreed. "I'm going to be a lot more
careful from now on."

"For sure," Lincoln said, nodding in agreement.

"Hey, let's play a game together," Fiery offered.

The other two looked at her and smiled.

"Why not?" Drudy answered with a smile.

"Let's be extra careful," Lincoln added.

"Also, let's not be competitive," Fiery concluded.

— ♦ —

"I'm glad that I didn't get into as much trouble as Drudy did," Tristan said when the story had ended.

"Yes, so am I," his grandfather said and smiled. "But it's very important to remember that accidents often happen when we're not careful, and also—as in Drudy's case—if we get competitive when we play with others, and always want to win."

"I guess I'd better tie my shoelaces, Grandpa, before I go play again," Tristan said.

"And before you go, there's one other thing you should remember that Drudy's story taught us. Can you remember what?"

Tristan put his hand on his chin and thought for a moment. "To pray?"

"That's right! Then God can protect you from getting hurt."

Tristan and his grandfather bowed their heads and said a little prayer. Then Tristan bounded off to play with his friend. On a nearby leaf, three small insects watched him and exchanged smiles.

Moral

Ask God to give you a helping hand when you need one, and He'll be there for you.

Lincoln's Lullaby

"Grandpa, will you tell me a bedtime story?" Tristan asked, as his grandfather tucked him into bed.

"Of course. I wonder what would be a good story to tell you," he said thoughtfully.

"Can you tell me another story about Drudy and her insect friends?" the little boy said. "I really like them."

"Aha, I just thought of a perfect bedtime story," Grandpa Jake replied. "It's about Lincoln, Drudy's ladybug friend. It also happened at bedtime."

"Goody!" Tristan exclaimed, and then settled down while his grandfather began the story.

"Late one night, when little children all over the neighborhood were safely tucked in their beds, a small group of insect friends were gathered together ..." Grandpa Jake began.

"Twinkle, twinkle, little star, how I wonder what you are!"

Lincoln sang, as he lay on a leaf, staring up at the starry night sky.

"Up above the world so high," Wallace joined in, and the two continued the chorus together, "Like a diamond in the sky."

Lincoln and Wallace sang the rest of the lullaby together. When it came to an end they were silent.

The air was very still and quiet around them. The soft trickle of the nearby stream could be heard clearly, as well as the rustle of the slight breeze whispering through the leaves of their tree. There were other noises as well— crickets chirping their nightly tune, hooting owls in search of dinner, the frogs croaking their melodious chorus, and the little footsteps of raccoons scurrying around looking for food.

Lincoln and Wallace listened to the night sounds and watched as the fireflies lit up and danced around the pond.

Then Lincoln sighed. "I wish I could write a lullaby," he said, sitting up and facing Wallace.

"Why don't you try?" Wallace asked.

"I don't think I can. I've never written a song before. But I love singing lullabies."

"You should try," Wallace encouraged. "I think you could write a beautiful lullaby."

"I guess I should give it a try, but..." Lincoln started, then his sentence trailed off. "I'll think about it."

The two friends said goodnight, and turned over on their leaves. Wallace was soon fast asleep; however, Lincoln stayed awake thinking about the lullaby he longed to write.

He pondered it a little longer, until he too joined Wallace in restful sleep.

I wonder if I could really write one, he thought. *I should probably try. But what if I can't do it— what then?*

The next day Lincoln flew off to a quiet spot. He decided that he was going to give songwriting a try. Finding the perfect blade of grass for composing, he settled down and was soon deep in thought.

"What should I write it about?—A star?" he thought aloud, and then shook his head. "The night animals?" He scrunched up his face, disliking the idea. "Hmmm, the dark? Night sounds?" Lincoln let out a distressed wail. "I can't even think of *what* to write my lullaby about; how am I ever going to even start?"

Discouraged that he could not accomplish what he so longed to, he exclaimed: "I'll never be good at anything! This is terrible; I should've never even tried."

Just then a
voice sounded
behind him. "There you are!
I've been looking for you." It was
Wallace.

By this time Lincoln was very distraught and
frustrated.

"What's wrong?" Wallace asked, noticing
Lincoln's unhappy face.

"Nothing," Lincoln muttered, not knowing how to
explain the problem.

"Could've fooled me. You look pretty down."
Wallace sat next to him and gave him a friendly
nudge.

Realizing that he couldn't
hide the obvious from his friend,
Lincoln shrugged and let out a sigh. "Actually,
something is wrong," he said. "Remember last night
when I said I wanted to write a lullaby?"

"Uh-huh," Wallace responded.

"After thinking about it some more, I decided that
I'd try and write one today."

"Wow, I'm sure it's going to be great," said
Wallace with a warm smile.

"I don't think so!" Lincoln frowned. "I couldn't
even think of what to write the lullaby about.
I tried and tried, but I didn't come up with
anything. I can't do it!" he concluded.

"Oh," his friend said. "I'm sorry about that, but you can't just give up; you have to keep trying. Sometimes you have to try over and over again until you get it right."

"But I can't!" Lincoln said, exasperated. "I won't be able to write a lullaby, ever!"

Wallace thought for a minute, and then turned to his distressed friend. "Did you pray and ask God to help you?" he finally said.

Lincoln looked down and shook his head.

"You should," Wallace said. "I'm sure He'd help you. Then, if you want, I could help you as well. I've never

written a lullaby before either. It will be a first for both of us, but we can do it together with God's help."

A smile spread across Lincoln's face. "I like that idea," he said. "You're a great friend, Wallace."

"That's such a nice thing for you to say. Come on, let's get started."

The two friends bowed their heads to pray.

"God, please cheer Lincoln up," Wallace prayed. "Help us now as we write this lullaby. Show us what to write this song about, and even give us the words for it. Also, help us to keep trying even when it doesn't seem to work. Amen."

"I thought of something," Lincoln said. "What if we wrote it about nighttime sounds?"

"I like that! What would you think about singing it for Drudy, Bits and Fiery once it's written?"

Lincoln nodded his head in agreement. "I think they'd like that."

Soon the words and tune to the lullaby started coming together. Every time Wallace and Lincoln got stuck, they would bow their heads and ask God to help them, and He did. Before long, they had their lullaby.

That night, in
the moonlight, Lincoln
and Wallace sang their
lullaby for their friends.
"That was beautiful!"
exclaimed Bits when they
were done. "I'd like to
learn to sing it, too."
Fiery nodded her
head, liking the
idea as well.
Lincoln couldn't have
been happier.

"That was a nice story," Tristan said, as Grandpa finished. "Do you think you could help me write a lullaby sometime, too?"

"I'd be happy to," Grandpa Jake answered. "And when we do, we can remember all the things that Lincoln and Wallace learned about not giving up and asking God to help them."

"Oh yes! I think it will be a good lullaby." Tristan smiled and then yawned. "Grandpa, before I fall asleep, could you sing Lincoln's lullaby for me?"

"Why, of course. Close your eyes and I'll sing it for you."

A Nighttime Lullaby

When darkness covers the sky,
And stars twinkle up on high,
I love to listen to all the sounds,
That nighttime brings around.

I hear the crickets' song;
The frogs also sing along.
Shhh, I can hear the breeze,
Rustling the grass and leaves.

Hush now, and listen well,
There's a nighttime tale
Told to all, near and far,
No matter where you are.

Wobbly Wallace

Hee, hee," Tristan giggled, as he walked up the stairs to the front porch of his home. There sat Grandpa Jake in his favorite rocking chair. Just as he did each evening, he was watching the sunset.

"You seem to be having fun, Tristan," Grandpa Jake said.

Tristan looked up and grinned. "Oh, I just saw the funniest thing!"

"So it seems," Grandpa Jake replied. "Tell me about it. What was so funny?"

"I was playing with my friend behind the house," Tristan began, "when we saw Derek from next door come out of his house. You wouldn't believe what happened!"

"Oh?" Grandpa Jake inquired, raising a curious eyebrow. "And what was that?"

"When Derek came out of the house he tripped and fell down the stairs. But the funny thing was that when he got up, his foot was stuck in a small bucket. He couldn't get his foot out of the bucket. He was pulling and pulling, trying to get it out. When he finally did, his shoe stayed stuck in the bucket."

By the end of his story, Tristan was laughing very hard, but his grandpa wasn't. Instead, a sad look came across Grandpa Jake's face.

"He could have been badly hurt! How do you think Derek felt when you and your friend were laughing at him?" Grandpa Jake asked.

Tristan looked at his grandpa. He was a little puzzled as he thought about that.

Grandpa Jake continued, "If you were in Derek's place, how would you feel if

someone started laughing when something unpleasant happened to you?"

"Not so good, I guess," Tristan said in a whisper. He stared at the ground.

"It usually doesn't feel very nice when people make fun of you, especially when you've had an accident. That reminds me of a story about Wallace."

Tristan's face lit up. "Please tell me!"

Wallace walked slowly along, pushing his way around the blades of grass. He was bent and he hobbled along, leaning hard on a twig for support. There was a bandage on his leg and a pained look on his face.

The day before, while collecting food for his dinner, Wallace had tripped over a dandelion root and injured his leg. Drudy had come to his rescue. She had gotten him all bandaged up and fed him some dinner too, so he wouldn't have to walk on his hurt leg.

FIRST AID

Today Wallace was feeling a bit better. He was able to hobble along with the help of a crutch, but he still felt pretty miserable.

"Why did I have to get all banged up?" he muttered to himself. "Now I have this big bandage on my leg and it hurts. I feel terrible! If only I hadn't tripped over that root, none of this would've happened."

Wallace limped slowly on. Suddenly his crutch snapped in two. Once again, Wallace landed in a heap on the ground.

"OUCH!" he cried.

"I didn't think things could get worse," he said angrily, "but now look at me. — I've fallen once again."

Poor Wallace!

Just then
he heard a snicker nearby.
Wallace turned and spotted two little
beetles sitting on a cloverleaf laughing.
They had been watching Wallace
hobble along through the grass, and
when his twig broke it looked so funny to
them that they laughed and laughed.
"Wallace is so clumsy," said Specks,
in between laughs.
The other beetle, Jibber,
started chanting, "Wobbly
Wallace!"

Specks joined in, and the two began singing that line over and over again.

Wallace stared at the ground. His sore leg hurt even more now, but what was worse was the hurt he felt inside. He wanted to cry. His eyes grew misty as the two beetles continued chanting.

I guess I really am wobbly and clumsy, Wallace thought sadly. *I seem to have a lot of accidents. And then after that, I have more accidents. I'm always hurting myself or spilling this or dropping that. I can't do anything!*

"Go away," he said sadly to Jibber and Specks. But the naughty beetles only laughed harder.

"Oh dear, what happened here?" It was Drudy. She hovered just above Wallace, with a concerned look on her face. "I guess that's what the shout I heard was all about," she said. "I'm so sorry that you fell again, Wallace."

Wallace didn't look up at Drudy; he continued to stare at the ground. He now had tears in his eyes.

"Are you okay, Wallace?" Drudy asked, wondering why her normally cheerful friend seemed so sad. She settled on a leaf near him. "Does it really hurt?" she asked.

Wallace nodded his head slightly.

It was then that Drudy

heard Jibber and Specks, still giggling and chanting nearby. She tilted her head to listen to them.

"Wobble … wobble … Wobbly Wallace!" they said, and then burst into laughter again.

The beetles hadn't noticed Drudy's arrival and were very surprised when they looked up to see the dragonfly hovering in front of them. There was a disappointed look on her face.

"Are you beetles having fun?" she asked.

Jibber and Specks stopped laughing and sat up straight. "Uh … uh," Specks stuttered.

"We just saw something very funny, that's all," Jibber said, and then giggled as she looked at Specks.

"When Wallace was walking, his crutch snapped," Jibber told Drudy. "It was so, so funny." And the two beetles laughed some more.

But Drudy wasn't laughing.

"You know what?" she said. "It may have looked pretty funny to you, but poor Wallace could've been badly hurt, and instead of finding out if he was okay, you just laughed at him. You can make someone feel very sad inside if you make fun of him when things go wrong."

The beetles looked thoughtfully at Wallace. Then, all of a sudden, the cloverleaf they had been sitting on gave in under their weight. The two beetles tumbled to the ground, rolling as they did.

Seeing the beetles rolling around in the soft grass was a rather funny sight, but instead of laughing, Drudy hurried over to Jibber and Specks and asked if they were all right.

"Oh dear, that was quite a fall," she said. "Are you hurt?"

"I'm okay," Specks said.

"Me too. Just a little tumble," added Jibber.

"I'm so glad you're not hurt," Drudy said, as she helped the beetles to their feet.

"I feel really bad about making fun of Wallace," Specks said, as he dusted himself off.

"Me too," Jibber said shyly. "We should go say we're sorry."

"And maybe we can help him with some things," Specks added. "That way he doesn't have to walk on his sore leg."

"That's so thoughtful of you two," Drudy said with a smile. "I'm sure Wallace would appreciate your kindness and help."

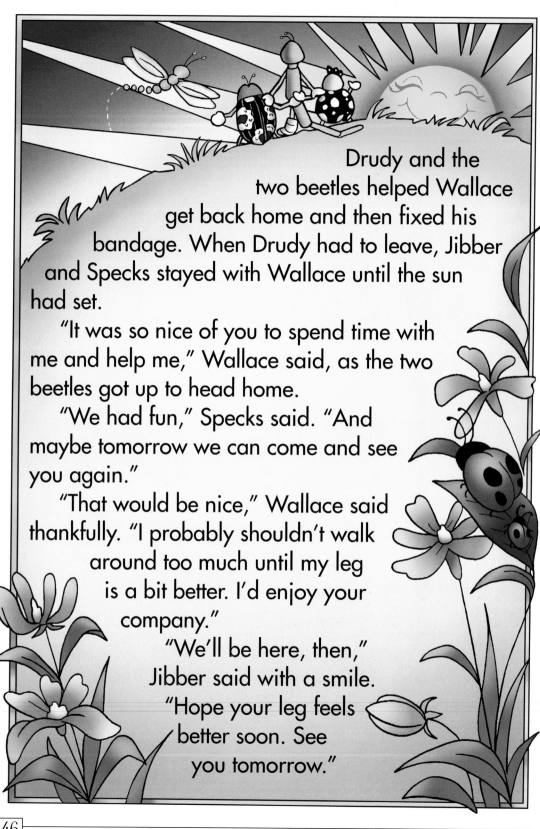

Drudy and the two beetles helped Wallace get back home and then fixed his bandage. When Drudy had to leave, Jibber and Specks stayed with Wallace until the sun had set.

"It was so nice of you to spend time with me and help me," Wallace said, as the two beetles got up to head home.

"We had fun," Specks said. "And maybe tomorrow we can come and see you again."

"That would be nice," Wallace said thankfully. "I probably shouldn't walk around too much until my leg is a bit better. I'd enjoy your company."

"We'll be here, then," Jibber said with a smile. "Hope your leg feels better soon. See you tomorrow."

"The end," Grandpa Jake read, closing his storybook.

"I feel badly about making fun of Derek," Tristan said thoughtfully after a moment's silence. "I'm going to try to be nicer to him and not laugh when things go wrong for him."

"That's excellent," Grandpa Jake said. "I'm sure he'll enjoy having you as a friend."

Firefly Flower

"You seem a little down today, Tristan. Is something wrong?" Grandpa Jake asked, when he saw his grandson sitting on the chair with a sad look on his face.

"My best friend, Kyle, is sick," Tristan answered. "His mommy says he has the mumps. And that I can't see him, because I could get sick too."

"I'm sorry," responded Grandpa Jake.

"But his mommy does have a point. It wouldn't be nice if you got sick, would it?"

"No. But I wanted to play with Kyle. It might make him feel better."

"I'm sure Kyle wants to play with you too. Sometimes, though, you have to choose to do the right thing, even if it's not what you'd prefer to do," Grandpa Jake explained. "You see, if you and Kyle played together now, while he's sick, he wouldn't be able to get the rest he needs in order to get better. You might also catch the mumps from him, and then you would have to be in bed for some time. That would be sad."

Grandpa Jake paused to let Tristan think about what he had just said.

"Grandpa, is there anything I can do to make Kyle feel better?" Tristan asked thoughtfully.

"That's an excellent question and a very nice thought.

"I think I might have a story that would help to answer that. It's about one time when Bits and Lincoln got sick."

"I feel so miserable,"
Bits said, as she lay curled
up in her bed.
"Me, too," Lincoln
agreed.

The day before, the two insects had been out a ways from their homes when they got caught in an unexpected thunderstorm. They tried to find shelter, but it was raining so heavily that the little leaves they had stood under couldn't protect them from the big raindrops. When Bits and Lincoln had gotten home they were both soaking wet.

By the next day they were both sick with a terrible cough and cold. They lay on two leaves, both feeling pretty miserable.

Oh deary me! Fiery thought, as she hovered a short distance away and saw poor Bits and Lincoln curled in their leaf beds. They look so sad. I want to go see them, but then I might get sick as well. I wish there was something I could do. God, please show me what I can do to make Lincoln and Bits feel better.

"What would make me feel better if I were sick?" Fiery asked herself aloud. "Why of course! Thank You, God, for that idea!"

A big smile came across her face. Fiery flew off in search of her other friends.

"I was thinking how nice it would be if we could do something to cheer up Bits and Lincoln," Fiery told her friends, who were now gathered together. "I had an idea of something that would be fun for them and for us, but I need your help. Does anybody want to help me cheer up our sick friends?"

"For sure!" the others chorused.

"Okay then! Everyone gather around, and listen to this plan. …"

A few minutes later, the little group excitedly went on their way to begin their preparations.

Nighttime had come. The moon was unusually bright, and hundreds of stars could be seen twinkling in the inky sky.

In the middle of a cough and a sneeze, Bits and Lincoln heard some rustling nearby.

"Did you hear something?" Bits asked Lincoln, after another sneeze.

"It's coming from my side over here," responded Lincoln. "I'll go see what it is."

Lincoln clambered out of his leaf and walked a few paces away from it. "Who's there?" he called.

But all he found was a little leaf with some writing on it. "'Presenting Firefly Flower,'" Lincoln read.

"What does that mean?" Bits asked, glad to have something to think about besides her aching throat.

"I don't know. Looks like it's the name of a show or something.

It's probably something we're missing out on because we're sick." "Probably," Bits agreed sadly.

Just then Fiery flew down.

"Hey there, Fiery!" Lincoln shouted out.

"Hi, Bits and Lincoln! Quickly hop back into bed, Lincoln, and the two of you get comfortable," Fiery said. "We have a surprise for you!"

"A surprise?" Bits asked curiously. "What sort of surprise?"

"You'll see," Fiery said, then flew out of sight.

"Oh, this is so exciting!" Lincoln exclaimed, climbing hurriedly back into his bed.

A minute passed and nothing happened. Then suddenly they heard the old bullfrog from the pond begin his song. A single firefly, all aglow, started dancing a short distance from them, to the bullfrog's song.

Another firefly began dancing along, and soon more joined in. Other frogs began to join the bullfrog's chorus too.

The fireflies danced and swayed to the beautiful chorus of the frogs, while Lincoln and Bits watched the whole show, clapping happily in time. They both felt so good inside, although they had been so miserable only minutes earlier. The fireflies made special flower-like formations in the air, and lit up at different times.

At the end of the show, Lincoln and Bits cheered and clapped. "Thank you so much!" they both exclaimed. "You made us feel a whole lot better," Lincoln said." That's for sure," agreed Bits.

The two little insects were snug in bed, just about ready to sleep. "We should do something special for our friends when we're better," Bits said to Lincoln.

"Yes," answered Lincoln with a yawn. "Maybe tomorrow we can plan it, seeing as we still have to stay in bed."

"Good idea. Sleep well, Lincoln," Bits said, as she turned over and shut her eyes.

"You too."

"Maybe I can make Kyle a 'get well' card so he knows that I miss him," Tristan said when the story had ended.

"I'm sure that would make him feel loved and remembered," Grandpa Jake agreed. "When you're finished making it, I'll walk you over to his house to deliver it. What do you think?"

"For sure. I'm going to make the card right now.

To Kyle

INK

"Thanks, Grandpa," Tristan said, as he walked excitedly into his room to find a paper and some colors.

Moral

There are always ways to cheer others up and make them happy. Ask God to show you what you can do to make someone smile and feel better.

That's mine! You can't have it!" Tristan shouted angrily, as he pulled a toy engine away from his cousin, Troy. "That's my special engine, and I want to play with it!"

"But I was playing with it first," Troy said, his eyes beginning to brim with tears. "It's not nice to grab."

"It's my favorite toy!" said Tristan. "And I don't want you to play with it."

"Those are not very kind words, Tristan." It was Grandpa Jake. He had heard the two boys shouting and had come to find out what the argument was about.

"Troy keeps taking all my favorite toys and playing with them," Tristan said.

"But he's not playing with them," Troy argued tearfully. "He just doesn't want me to play with them."

"Is that so, Tristan?" Grandpa Jake asked. "Why wouldn't you want Troy to play with your toys?"

"Because…," Tristan answered, pausing momentarily, "I *might* want to play with them and if he's playing with them then I can't."

"This reminds me of a story," Grandpa Jake said, rubbing his chin thoughtfully.

"What's the story about?" Troy asked, as he dried his tears.

"Well, if I remember correctly, Bits was also having a hard time sharing with others," Grandpa Jake said. "Let me get my storybook. Maybe we can learn something that will help solve this problem."

It was not a good day for Bits. She wore a constant frown as she busied herself around the hive. Something was definitely bothering her. All morning Bits had felt sad and angry.

As she flew out of the hive to collect some more nectar, she heard someone calling her.

"Bits! Wait up!" It was Pepper, one of her friends from a nearby hive.

Bits slowed down momentarily. She felt grumpy and wasn't sure that she wanted Pepper's company right now.

Panting a little as he caught up to her, Pepper smiled. "Phew, you're sure flying around fast today, Bits. Helps an old bee like me keep in shape," Pepper said with a chuckle.

Bits gave a slight smile. "I really must hurry along," she said. "I have to collect more nectar."

She was anxious to be on her way again and didn't feel like talking with anyone.

"Mind if I buzz along with you?" Pepper asked.

"I guess so, if you'd like," Bits answered, as she hurried on.

They flew to the next patch of flowers, full of juicy nectar that Bits would take back to the hive and which the other bees would then use to make honey.

Pepper chattered constantly, but Bits didn't offer much to the conversation.

"It's such a beautiful day!" Pepper exclaimed, as he paused and lay on a blade of grass.

Bits only shrugged.

"Oh, I enjoy the summer so much!" Pepper went on.

Once again, Bits didn't say anything.

Finally Pepper sat up and looked at Bits, who was furiously collecting nectar. "What's bothering you, Bits?"

"Nothing," she replied.

"Well, you haven't said more than a few words to me today. I can't help but notice that you seem to be somewhat angry." Pepper paused. "You're not angry at me, are you?"

Bits finally stopped hurrying about the place. "Oh no, not at all!" she said, suddenly feeling very bad for the way she'd been ignoring Pepper. "I'm sorry, Pepper. You haven't done anything to make me angry with you. I've just been having a bit of a bummer day."

"I can understand that. Bummer days are never fun," Pepper sympathized. "Did something happen?"

"You could say that," Bits said, as she settled on the blade of grass next to Pepper. "A few days ago, after we had just finished making a whole stash of delicious honey, the farmer came by and took well over half of the honey we had made. We had all spent days and days going out and collecting nectar to make the honey, and then he just came and took it. That wasn't the first time that has happened either. He comes and takes our honey quite often.

"I didn't mind so much before," she continued. "It's not that he takes all of it, and there's always enough left for us, but it just makes me angry at times because I have to work so hard for it."

"Hmmm, I can understand how that would be frustrating," Pepper said softly. "I once felt the same way, back at my hive."

"You did?" Bits asked in surprise. "Does it still bother you?"

"No, because I found out something very interesting," he answered. "Do you know why the farmer takes the honey, Bits?"

"Uh-uh!" she said, shaking her head.

"Well, the farmer uses the honey too, just like we do. The farmer finds honey so delicious that he takes some so that he can eat it with his pancakes, or on bread, or make other sweets out of it."

"Really?" Bits asked.

"Yes, he really thinks it's yummy. So does his little girl," Pepper added with a smile.

Bits thought for a moment. "I guess it's not so bad that he takes our honey. I never knew that it was because he liked it so much."

"Giving to others, even of something that we like or have worked hard to make, makes God happy," Pepper explained. "Because no matter what we give, we always get more in return. God likes us to share with others, just like He shares the wonderful world He created with us."

"Thank you so much for explaining that to me, Pepper," Bits said, as she hugged him. "I'm sorry that I was such a grump this morning. What you told me has helped me to not get bitter about the fact that the farmer takes our honey. I feel much better now."

"Not a problem at all," Pepper said, returning her hug. "I'm glad I could help cheer you up!"

Later that day as Bits was collecting more nectar, she saw the farmer's little girl playing in the garden. The little girl heard Bits buzzing by, and she smiled. "Oh, thank You, God, for bees!" she exclaimed. "Honey is so yummy. Thank You for teaching them how to make it. And thank You that they share it with us."

Bits grinned from ear to ear. It made her glad inside to hear how happy the honey had made the little girl. "You're welcome," she whispered, as she flew back to her hive.

"I want to share my toys with you, Troy!" Tristan said. "Just like Bits was happy to give the honey she had worked hard to make, to the farmer and his family."

"Thank you," Troy said. "I'll be sure to take good care of them."

Grandpa Jake smiled as he left the room while the two boys went on happily playing together.

Moral

Giving to others makes you happy, because as you give to others, God is able to give to you.

Christmas Cheer

"Grandpa, do you have any Christmas stories about the insect friends?" Tristan asked.

"I believe I do," answered Grandpa Jake. "I'll have to check my storybook, though. Would you please get it for me?"

"Oh, sure!" the little boy exclaimed, as he bounded up the stairs in search of his grandpa's favorite storybook. He returned with the book and sat next to his grandpa, eager for a story.

"Ah, here it is: 'Christmas Cheer'!" Grandpa Jake said with a smile. He began to read….

It was a sunny winter day. Snow had fallen the night before, covering the ground in a soft, white blanket. Several insects hurriedly made their way to a gathering that had been called, leaving their little prints zigzagging in the snow.

Soon the insect friends had all arrived at the meeting spot, a homey underground burrow. They snuggled close together to keep warm.

"I was thinking," began Wallace, "how nice it would be if we could do something for our neighbors this Christmas."

"That sounds like fun!" Drudy exclaimed.

"What were you thinking of?" asked Lincoln.

"I'm not really sure," Wallace answered. "I haven't been able to think of anything yet. That's why I asked all of you to come, so that we could talk about it. Any ideas?"

"Hmmm, Christmas is supposed to be a time of giving," Bits said thoughtfully.

"And singing," chorused Specks and Jibber.

"I knew we'd come up with some good ideas," Wallace said with a smile.

"So what do we do next?" asked Jibber.

There was a moment of silence.

Finally Lincoln said thoughtfully: "I was just thinking, Christmas is Jesus' birthday, isn't it? I wonder what Jesus would want us to do for His birthday?"

"Maybe we should ask Him," Wallace suggested.

The others nodded.

So the eight insects bowed their heads and prayed. Once they had finished, they went back to planning their Christmas neighborhood event.

"Silent night, holy night," Lincoln sang in a shaky voice, and then let out a sigh. "I can't do it! My voice isn't good enough."

"Don't give up now," Jibber said, "you just have to keep practicing. Specks, come join us."

The three insects began the song again, together this time. After a few tries their voices blended beautifully as they sang:

Silent night, holy night!
All is calm, all is bright,
Round yon virgin mother
and child
Holy infant, so tender
and mild,
Sleep in heavenly peace,
Sleep in heavenly peace.

"That was wonderful!" exclaimed Drudy, as she and the other insects clapped enthusiastically.

"Oh, wow!" exclaimed Specks. "Those Christmas baskets are beautiful!"

"They really are," Lincoln agreed.

Lined on the ground were several baskets filled with presents, delicious snacks, and decorated with holly leaves and berries.

"Everyone has been working hard on them, and they really are excellent," Wallace said, as he peeked up from the leaf he was writing on.

"What are you doing, Wallace?" Bits asked.

"I've been putting together a list of all the insect families in our neighborhood that we could distribute the baskets to," he explained.

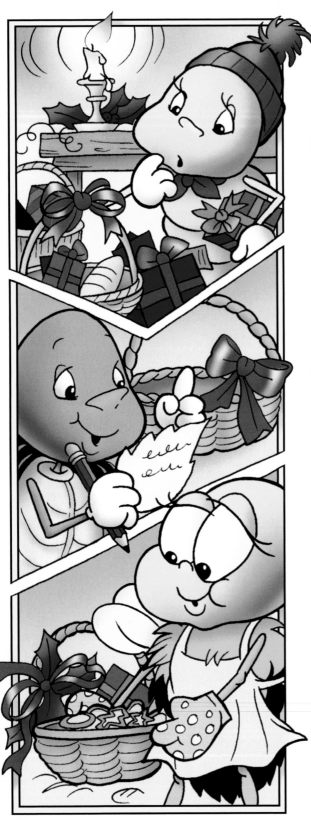

"How many do you have?" Drudy asked.

"About twelve."

"That means we're pretty much done," Jibber said, after counting the baskets. "Only two more to go."

"I'm so happy we could finish them up in time," Bits said. "It's Christmas Eve, and tonight we can distribute them."

"I'm so excited! I can't wait to get started!" Lincoln said eagerly.

Wallace thought of a plan. "How about if we all just finish up with the last two baskets, then we can all get ready for visiting?"

"Good idea," the insects chorused, and then got right to work.

Little snowflakes tumbled gently from the sky. As the insects walked, the snow crunched under their feet. The eight softly sang, "Joy to the world, the Lord is come… ."

They arrived at Mr. and Mrs. Beetle's place.

"Good evening, Mr. and Mrs. Beetle," Wallace greeted them.

"Good evening to you too, Wallace," Mr. Beetle replied. "And a merry Christmas to all of you!"

"Merry Christmas," said Mrs. Beetle. "What brings you here?"

"We wanted to give you
something special for Christmas,"
Drudy explained. "We brought you a
Christmas basket, and we'd like to sing
you a Christmas carol, if you'd like."

"How delightful!" Mrs. Beetle exclaimed.
"That's so thoughtful of you."

"We'd love to hear a carol," said Mr. Beetle,
and their two little beetle children nodded.

Lincoln began singing: "Silent night, holy night." The
others joined in, even Mr. and Mrs. Beetle.

When the song had ended, Mrs. Beetle gave each of
the insects a hug. "Thank you so much for visiting us,"

she said. "You have helped to make this a wonderful Christmas."

"Merry Christmas!" the eight insects called out as they went on their way to their next stop.

And on they went through the evening, bringing joy and happiness wherever they went, and a smile to the face of each one they met. At the end of the evening the eight said goodbye to each other before they headed off to their own homes.

"That was the best Christmas ever," Bits said.

"For sure," the others agreed together.

"I'd like to do something like that for Christmas," Tristan said when the story had ended. "But what could I do?"

"Good question," Grandpa Jake said. "Maybe you can do something for Derek next door, or you could make a Christmas card for your parents. There are so many things you can do for others. You can ask God to show you what to do for people. I'm sure He'd have some good ideas."

"I'll do that," Tristan said, bowing his head to pray.

It was to be the best Christmas for Tristan, because he was doing what Jesus likes best for His birthday: Tristan was thinking about others and how to make them happy.

Moral

The best Christmas present you can give to others is love and kindness. When you make others happy, you also make God happy.

Morals highlighted in
Insects Galore

In an animated and fun format, each story in *Insects Galore* focuses on one of these character-building morals:

- Ask God to give you a helping hand when you need one, and He'll be there for you. (From "Drudy's Day")

- It's important to keep trying, no matter how difficult or impossible something may seem. If you ask God to help, He'll be there for you. (From "Lincoln's Lullaby")

- Do to others what you would want them to do to you. As you do, you'll find out how much you get in return. (From "Wobbly Wallace")

- There are always ways to cheer others up and make them happy. Ask God to show you what you can do to make someone smile and feel better. (From "Firefly Flower")

- Giving to others makes you happy, because as you give to others, God is able to give to you. (From "Bitter, Better Bee")

- The best Christmas present you can give to others is love and kindness. When you make others happy, you also make God happy. (From "Christmas Cheer")

GRANDPA JAKE'S STORYBOOK

Crew and Co.

Come along with a team of hard-working construction vehicles including Dee the Dump truck, Lorry Loader, Crank Crane, the Con Crete Brothers and cheery Digger. Working together under wise Mr. Oversite, they each play an important part in completing the crew and getting the job done.

- ✓ Seeing a job through
- ✓ Following instructions
- ✓ Doing the right thing
- ✓ Resolving arguments
- ✓ Helping others
- ✓ Working as a team

Dino Tales

A group of dinosaur friends live a happy life together, filled with adventure and opportunities to show their concern for one another. When Crispin accidentally ruins his sister Dixie's garden, they and their friends work together to repair what's been damaged. Wesley's bedtime blues turn into a misadventure, but one with lessons worth having learned. A surprise invitation presents Bumble with the challenge of brushing up on manners fit for a banquet.

- ✓ Thinking about others
- ✓ Courtesy
- ✓ Healthy habits
- ✓ Obedience
- ✓ Honesty
- ✓ Resolving conflict
- ✓ Forgiveness